COOL CAT

by Michael Anthony Steele
Art by Mike Collins, Lee Loughridge,
and David Roach

BATMAN created by Bob Kane

SCHOLASTIC INC.

New York   Toronto   London   Auckland   Sydney
Mexico City   New Delhi   Hong Kong   Buenos Aires

ISBN 0-439-83002-8

Designed by Rick DeMonico

12 11 10 9 8 7 6 5 4 3 2 1   6 7 8 9 10/0

Printed in the U.S.A.
First printing, October 2006

In Gotham City, the night usually belongs to Batman. But on this particular night, Bruce Wayne's Batsuit was at home. Wayne was taking the night off to attend the party of his friend and fellow millionaire, Leo King.

"What do you think, Bruce?" asked Leo King. "The Feline Diamond is truly the jewel of my cat collection."

"Hello, Leo," said Catwoman as she leaped into the room and snatched the diamond. "This is purrrrr-fect for *my* collection."

King tried to stop her but she shoved him away. During the scuffle, a lamp smashed against the frozen tiger's case, shattering the ice.

Catwoman quickly escaped.
Meanwhile, electricity from the lamp
revived the ancient tiger. It burst from
the ice and lunged toward Leo King.

"Oh, excuse me, Leo," said Bruce. He pretended to stumble into King, pushing him to safety. The tiger darted past the other guests and bounded out the front door.

Bruce quickly ducked out of the party. He followed the tiger down the stairs and out the building. Using the Batwave, he summoned the Batmobile. It was time to become Batman!

The Batmobile zoomed after the tiger. Both the cat and the bat dodged heavy traffic. Batman knew the city was no place for a wild animal. He couldn't let the tiger hurt itself or anyone else.

Batman slammed on the brakes as the tiger disappeared into a narrow alley. He opened the hatch and fired his grappler into the air. He'd have to chase this cat from the rooftops.

Batman felt a sting around his neck. It was the end of Catwoman's whip! She jerked him backward.

"Hello, Batman," she purred. "I didn't expect you to find me so quickly."

The two battled across Gotham's rooftops.

"I don't have time for this," Batman growled. "King's saber-toothed tiger is loose!"

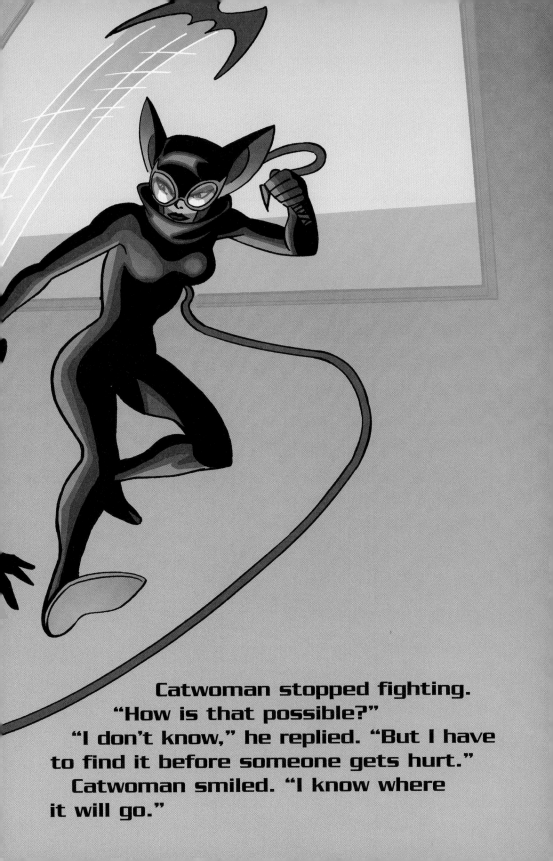

Catwoman stopped fighting.
"How is that possible?"
"I don't know," he replied. "But I have
to find it before someone gets hurt."
Catwoman smiled. "I know where
it will go."

Catwoman led Batman to a street filled with restaurants.

"To catch a cat, you have to think like one," she said. "That tiger has been frozen for ten thousand years. It must be hungry."

While Catwoman whisked two people to safety, Batman dove for the tiger. He tackled the giant beast, and together they tumbled down the sidewalk.

Batman tried to fight the saber-toothed tiger without hurting it. Unfortunately, the giant cat quickly pinned him.

"Here, kitty, kitty, kitty," said Catwoman, trying to distract the tiger.

Then Batman had an idea. He activated the Batwave.

The Batmobile roared toward them. Batman thought this was the perfect time to test his newest invention. He pressed another button on his belt. A large net blasted from the car, snaring the big cat.

"Don't worry," Batman told the tiger. "They'll feed you well at the Gotham Zoo."

He turned and saw Catwoman scrambling up a nearby building. He fired his grappler toward the rooftops. Batman still had one more cat to catch.

Batman swung onto the rooftop.
"Thanks for your help," he said.
"Now hand over the diamond."

Catwoman hissed and dove toward him. This time, the cat tackled *him*. They tumbled across the rooftop.

Catwoman broke free and dove off the rooftop. "This cat has nine lives, remember?"

Batman let her go. Luckily, he had snatched the diamond out of her bag. Batman was glad he had caught two out of three cats that night.